Callipidder Birds

Judy Steiner Grin

Judy Steiner Grin

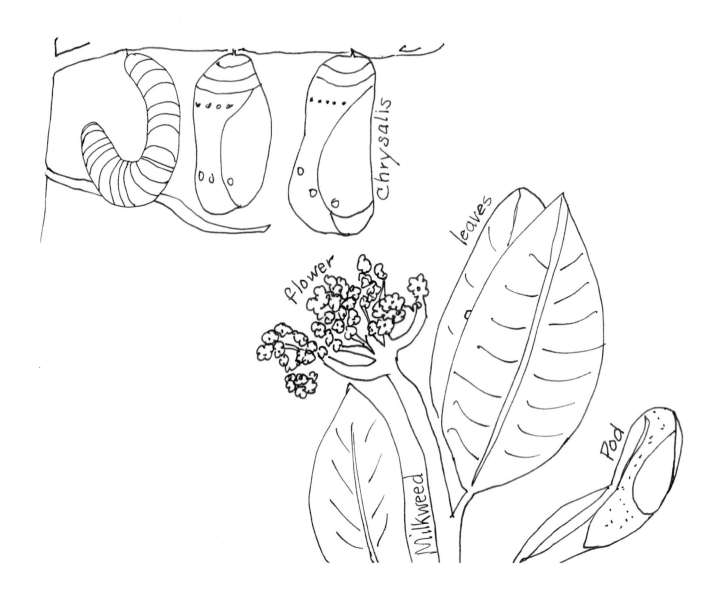

ISBN-13: 978-1975718749
ISBN-1975718747
LCCN: 2017914017
CreateSpace Independent Publishing Platform
North Charleston, SC

For all my children, real and pretend.

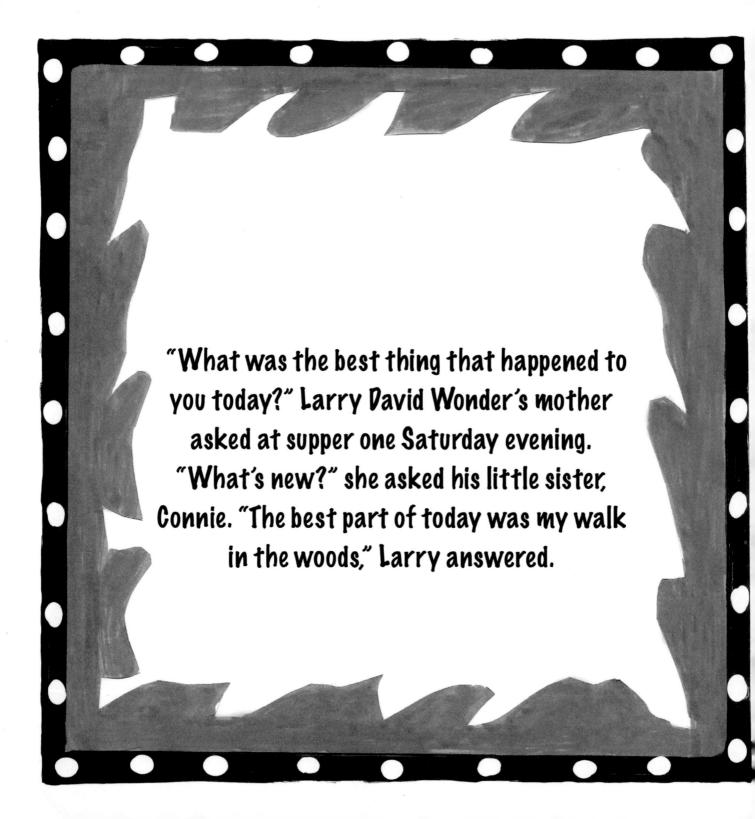

"What was the best thing that happened to you today?" Larry David Wonder's mother asked at supper one Saturday evening. "What's new?" she asked his little sister, Connie. "The best part of today was my walk in the woods," Larry answered.

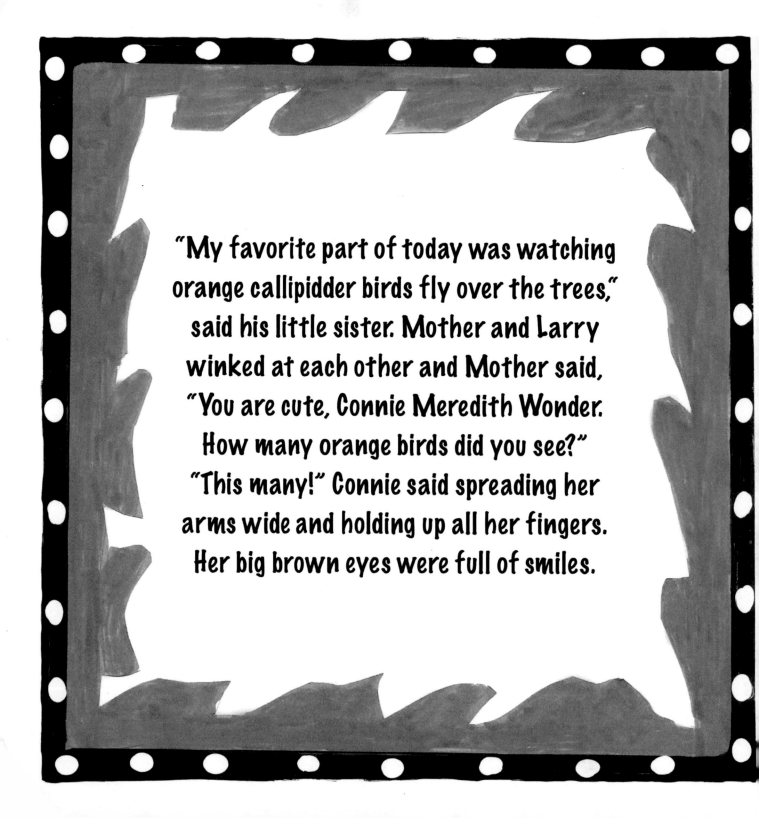

"My favorite part of today was watching orange callipidder birds fly over the trees," said his little sister. Mother and Larry winked at each other and Mother said, "You are cute, Connie Meredith Wonder. How many orange birds did you see?" "This many!" Connie said spreading her arms wide and holding up all her fingers. Her big brown eyes were full of smiles.

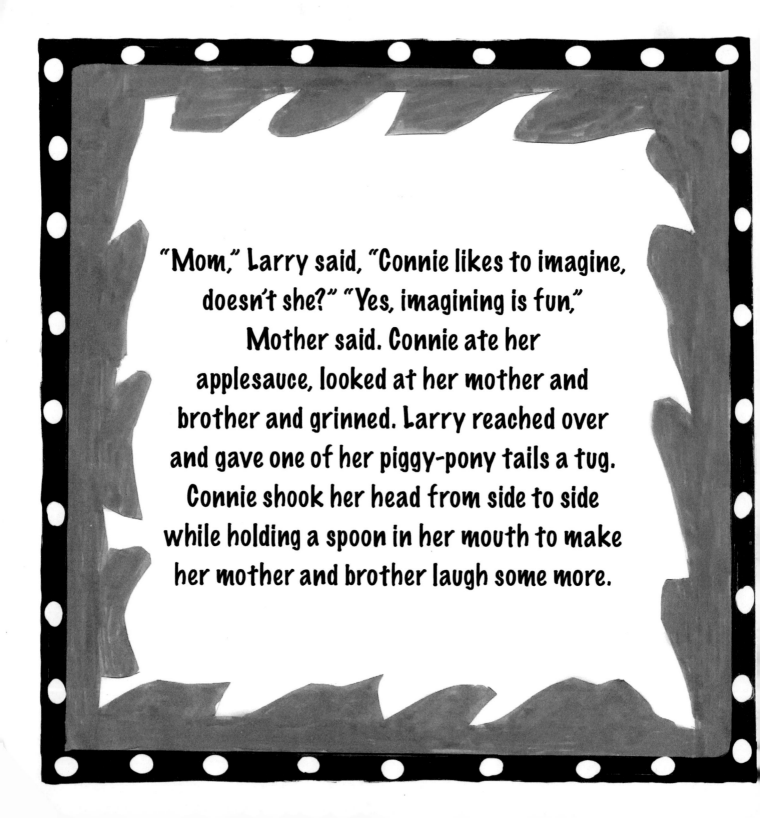

"Mom," Larry said, "Connie likes to imagine, doesn't she?" "Yes, imagining is fun," Mother said. Connie ate her applesauce, looked at her mother and brother and grinned. Larry reached over and gave one of her piggy-pony tails a tug. Connie shook her head from side to side while holding a spoon in her mouth to make her mother and brother laugh some more.

The next morning there were no friends to play with and Larry had already used his building blocks to make everything he could think of, so he decided to take another walk in the woods. "Want to come with me?" Larry asked his sister. He grabbed his collecting jar and waited for her answer. "I'll come," Connie said, putting her crayon down. "I want to see the callipidder birds again."

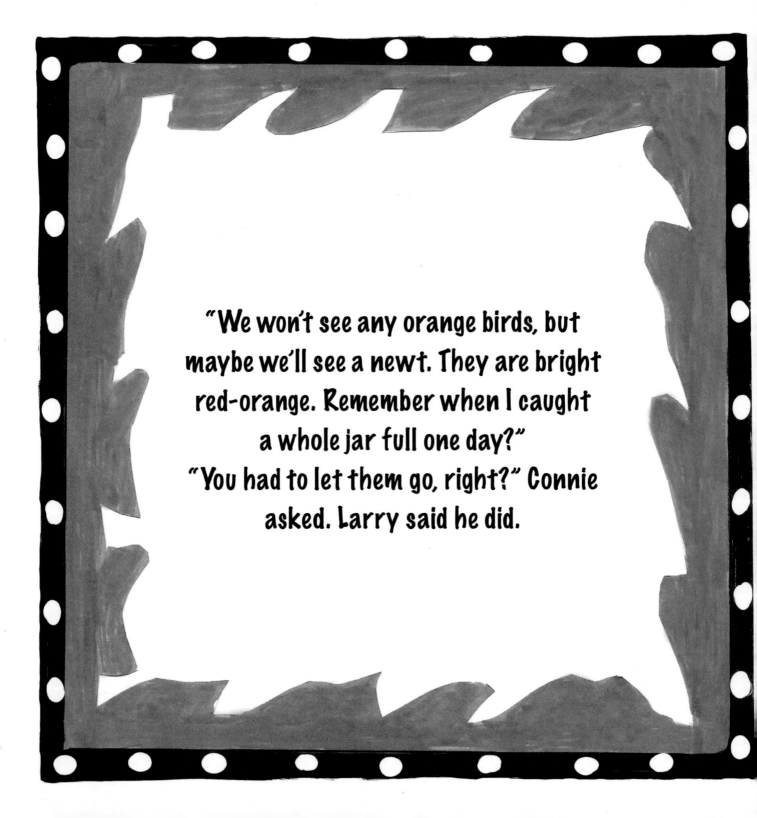

"We won't see any orange birds, but maybe we'll see a newt. They are bright red-orange. Remember when I caught a whole jar full one day?"
"You had to let them go, right?" Connie asked. Larry said he did.

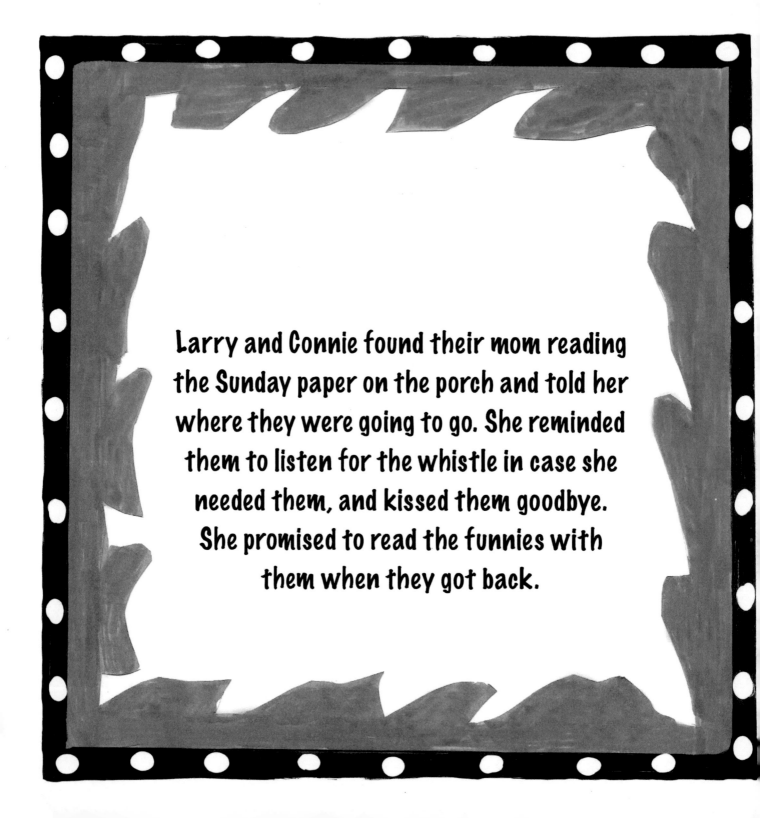

Larry and Connie found their mom reading the Sunday paper on the porch and told her where they were going to go. She reminded them to listen for the whistle in case she needed them, and kissed them goodbye. She promised to read the funnies with them when they got back.

Connie followed her brother down the path toward the creek. They found sticks to poke at dried leaves on the ground, and began looking for small creatures to take home in the jar. After they had looked for a while, Larry found a snail. Connie found a bright yellow spider. "I didn't know spiders could be yellow," Larry said.

"I did," said Connie, "and birds can be orange too. At least callipidder ones."

Larry helped Connie put the spider in a jar, but didn't say anything about orange birds. They walked a while looking for whatever they could find. Larry walked faster than Connie, and had to wait for her to catch up. Connie was looking up and over and all around, while Larry had his eyes on the ground. "Look, Larry, orange birds!" Connie said suddenly, shouting and pointing in front of her.

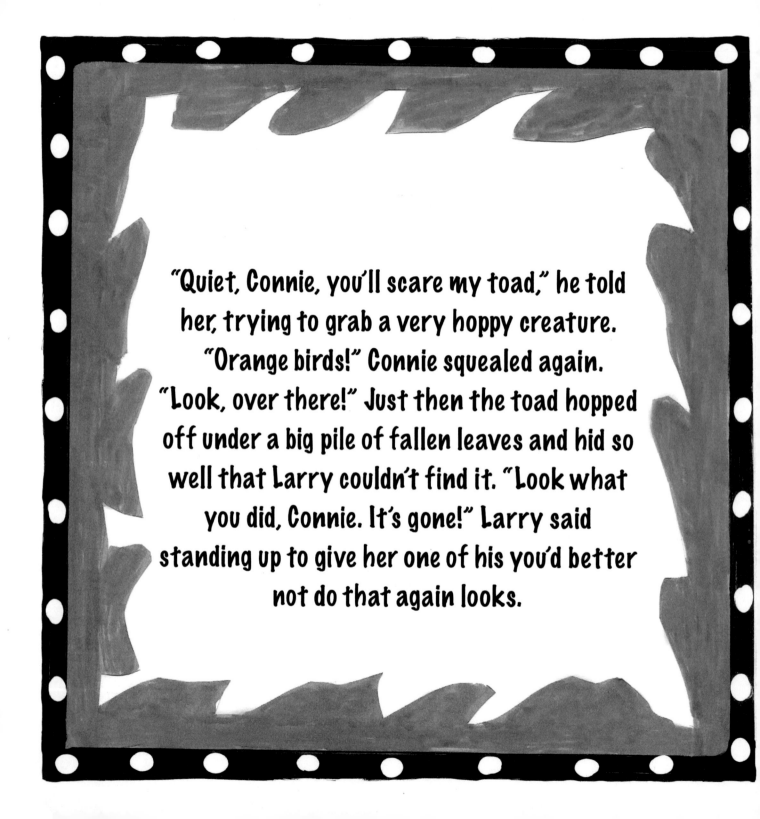

"Quiet, Connie, you'll scare my toad," he told her, trying to grab a very hoppy creature. "Orange birds!" Connie squealed again. "Look, over there!" Just then the toad hopped off under a big pile of fallen leaves and hid so well that Larry couldn't find it. "Look what you did, Connie. It's gone!" Larry said standing up to give her one of his you'd better not do that again looks.

He didn't see her right away. She wasn't behind him on the path. "Connie?" he said, turning around. "Look," she said. "Orange callipidder birds. This many!" She spread her arms and fingers wide again like she had the night before.

Larry finally saw where she was and where she was pointing and noticed a tree full of orange wings. Some were flapping slowly, and some were still and folded. "It looks like the leaves are alive," he said. "Callipidder birds! See Larry?" Connie said, going closer. "Stop, Connie, they might fly away." Larry stood near Connie and put his arm around her shoulder. "They are pretty, Connie, and they are orange, and they have wings. They even fly south for the winter, but they aren't birds."

"Don't they come from callipidders?"
Connie asked. "Well, if you put it that
way!" Larry said. "I get it. But you don't
call them birds. They're butterflies.
You found monarchs."
"Let's tell Mommy," Connie said.
"She can take a picture."

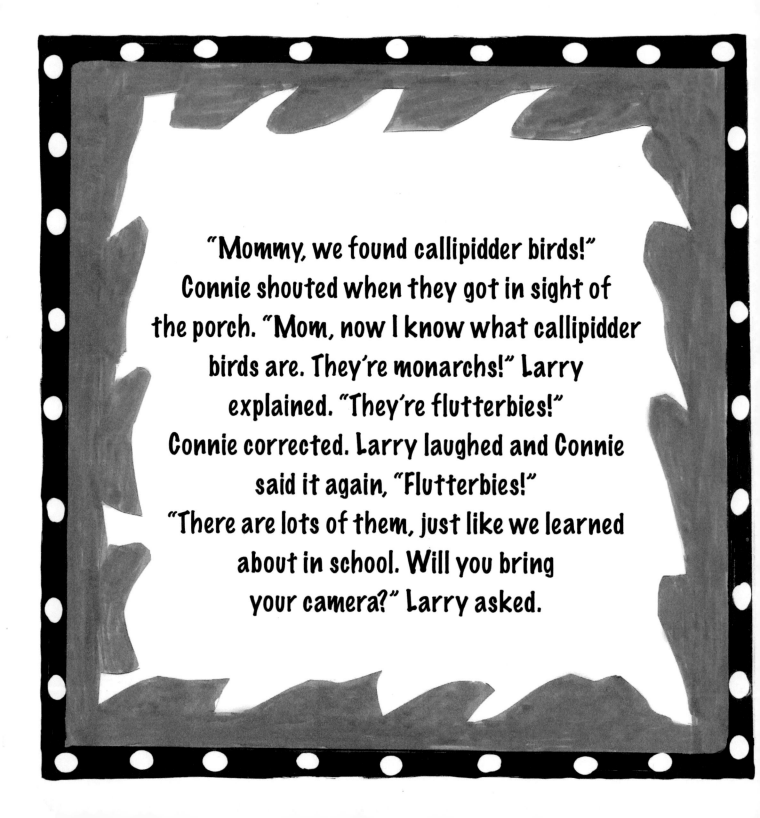

"Mommy, we found callipidder birds!" Connie shouted when they got in sight of the porch. "Mom, now I know what callipidder birds are. They're monarchs!" Larry explained. "They're flutterbies!" Connie corrected. Larry laughed and Connie said it again, "Flutterbies!" "There are lots of them, just like we learned about in school. Will you bring your camera?" Larry asked.

Mother took a picture just before the monarchs flew away toward the south. Then Mother, Larry and Connie walked happily home. Every once in a while Connie would say the words, "callipidder" and "flutterby" and they would all laugh together knowing exactly what she meant.

The next week, Larry David Wonder took the picture of the monarchs to first grade to show his class. He took a picture of Connie Meredith Wonder with him, too. After all, she was the first to discover that callipidder birds are really flutterbies.

A a B b C c D d E e F f G g H h I i J j K  P p Q q R r S s T t U u V v W w X x Y y Z z

A Caterpillar

Becomes a Butterfly

Migration Routes

Made in the USA
Middletown, DE
24 October 2017